Dawn Drew

5-C

Enid Blyton's

MR MEDDLE'S
MISCHIEF

First published 1970
This reprint 1988

Published by Dean, an imprint of
The Hamlyn Publishing Group Limited
Michelin House, 81 Fulham Road,
London SW3 6RB, England.

Copyright © Darrell Waters Limited 1940

ISBN 0 603 03276 1

Printed in Great Britain
at The Bath Press, Avon

Enid Blyton's
MR MEDDLE'S
MISCHIEF

DEAN

CONTENTS

CHAPTER I

MISTER MEDDLE'S MORNING

Mister Meddle was a pixie who couldn't mind his own business. He was for ever poking his long nose into other people's houses, and meddling with whatever they were doing.

One day he felt more meddlesome than usual, so he ran round to Dame Gladsome's. She was very busy that morning, but as soon as she saw Mister Meddle's nose round the door she flew to shut it!

"I've come to help you," said Meddle crossly.

"Oh, I'm much too busy to be bothered with your help!" said Dame Gladsome, and she turned the key in the lock.

Mister Meddle frowned and went to Old Man Twinkle, who was on the top of a ladder beside his big bookcase, turning out all his old books and dusting them.

"I'd like to help you," said Meddle, putting his head in at the window. He gave Old Man Twinkle such a fright that he fell off his ladder and bounced on to the table, sending his books up into the air.

Meddle decided not to wait and see what Old Man Twinkle said. He ran off and came to a neat little house on the top of the hill. It belonged to Mother Heyho. Meddle didn't know her very well. He knocked at her door.

Mother Heyho opened it. She had a handkerchief tied round her head

and a duster in her hand.

"Good morning," said Meddle politely. "Is there anything I can do for you? I happened to be passing, and as I had nothing much to do to-day, I wondered if I could be any help to you."

"How nice of you!" said Mother Heyho, who didn't know what a nuisance Mister Meddle could be. "Well, I badly want some butter and some eggs. Could you fetch some for me?"

Meddle was off like a shot. He went to the dairy, got the butter and eggs, and ran back with them. Mother Heyho opened the door. Meddle rushed in, but unfortunately he didn't notice that Mother Heyho had just polished the floor. He slid on a mat, turned head-over-heels— and the bag of eggs went flying to the ceiling and came down, smack, on Mother Heyho's head!

Mother Heyho was not at all pleased. Meddle put the butter carefully down on a chair and rubbed

his bruises.

"Anyway, the butter's not broken, like the eggs," he said.

"Don't be silly," said Mother Heyho, trying to get the eggs off her hair. "Butter doesn't break— but if it did, you'd have broken it! Now I shall have to wash my hair."

"I'll help you," said Meddle eagerly. He fetched a bowl for Mother Heyho and filled it full of water. Mother Heyho began to wash her hair. "Get me some more hot water," she said. "There's some in that kettle. Put it into a jug for me to pour over my hair."

Meddle emptied the water into a jug. Then he thought it would be very helpful if he poured the water over Mother Heyho's hair himself. So he tilted up the jug and poured.

"Oooh! Ow! Oooh!" yelled poor Mother Heyho, jumping almost up to the ceiling in fright. "It's boiling hot, you silly fellow! I'm cooked, I'm cooked!"

Meddle was horrified. He looked at Mother Heyho jumping round the kitchen, holding her hot head. He ran to the tap and drew some cold water. He threw it over Mother Heyho's hair.

"Ooooh! It's icy-cold!" shouted Mother Heyho. "Stop it! Leave me alone!"

Meddle tried to put the jug on the table and just missed it. Crash! It fell on to the floor and broke.

"My best milk-jug, oh, my best milk-jug!" wept Mother Heyho, in despair.

"Sorry," said Meddle. "I'll get some glue and mend it."

He ran to the store cupboard and found a little bottle of glue. Then back he went to mend the milk-jug. He put the glue on the table and picked up the milk-jug bits. But just as he was pressing them to-gether his hand slipped—and he knocked the glue-bottle off the table! The glue poured out on to the chair, the table, and the floor! Oh, what a mess!

Mother Heyho was busy drying her hair and didn't see what had happened. Meddle picked up the glue-bottle, but he couldn't pick up the glue!

The next thing that happened, of course, was that Meddle stepped straight into the sticky glue! His shoes stuck to the floor, and when he tried to get away his feet slipped out of his shoes, and there he was, dancing about in his socks! And, of course, the next thing he did was to dance right on to the glue again!

This time, when he tried to get out of it his socks came off, and there he was, in his bare feet!

Mother Heyho put her towel down at that moment and saw Meddle rushing about in bare feet. She was most astonished.

"Why have you taken your shoes

15

and stockings off?" she asked. "Do you think you're going to bed or something?"

Mother Heyho put her towel down on the gluey table, and glared at Meddle. She was getting tired of him. When she tried to pick the towel up she couldn't—it had stuck! She pulled in surprise.

"Let *me* help!" said Meddle at once, and he gave an enormous tug at the towel. It came up—and so did the table! Meddle sat down hurriedly on the floor, and the table fell on top of him, and a corner of it went on to Mother Heyho's toe.

How she yelled! She danced round the kitchen on one leg, holding her toe, whilst Meddle pushed away the table and tried to get up. The gluey

towel had got round his neck and he couldn't get it off.

"Oh, you wicked fellow!" cried Mother Heyho. "Look at all the mess and muddle you've made! Look at all the damage you've done! Now don't you dare to do another thing! Sit down and don't dare to move!"

Mother Heyho looked so fierce that Mister Meddle thought he had better do as he was told. So he sat down, squish, on a chair! But Mother Heyho only yelled at him all the more.

"Oh, you bad fellow! Oh, you silly pixie! Now you've sat on my butter! Get up, get up! You're sitting on my butter, I tell you! You've broken my eggs—and messed my hair—and nearly cooked my head—and broken my milk-jug—and got glue

18

over everything — and hurt my toe — and now you must sit on my butter! What else will you do, I'd like to know?"

Mister Meddle was frightened. He got up off the butter, and tried to go to the door in his bare feet. He could see Dame Gladsome and Old Man Twinkle going by outside.

"I can see two friends of mine," he said to Mother Heyho. "I must go."

"Well, I'll help you to go!" said Mother Heyho fiercely, and she caught up her big broom. Swish — swish — swish! She swept poor Meddle right off his feet, and he shot down the garden path and through the gate in a fearful hurry. He landed just under Old Man Twinkle's feet and gave him a fright.

"My goodness, it's Mister Meddle again!" said Dame Gladsome. "Is this the way you usually come out of a house, my dear Meddle? It seems very sudden."

Mister Meddle didn't answer. He rushed home in his bare feet, and got into a hot bath to get off all the glue. But it won't be long before he meddles again with somebody. He just simply can't help it!

CHAPTER II

MISTER MEDDLE AND THE CONJURER

Did you ever hear how Mister Meddle meddled with a conjurer one day? You didn't?—well, I'll tell you.

Now, you know, at some parties there is a conjurer who does all kinds of marvellous magic things. Well, once Meddle was invited to one of these parties, and he went, dressed up in his best suit, and feeling all excited.

There was a lovely tea—and afterwards there was to be the conjurer, doing magic tricks. Meddle didn't say a word all through his tea, because he was wondering and wondering how the conjurer would do his

21

magic. He guessed it must be because of his magic wand.

"Please go and play Nuts in May whilst I get the room ready for the conjurer," said Mrs. Twinkle, who was giving the party. So every one went into the next room, and soon they were singing, "Here we come gathering Nuts in May!"

But Mister Meddle wasn't. No— he had slipped into the tiny room where he had seen the conjurer put his coat and hat and bag, just to see if he could find anything interesting!

The bag was open! Some of the things were unpacked. The conjurer was not there. He was helping Mrs. Twinkle to arrange the chairs, so Meddle had the little room to

himself.

He looked for the magic wand. It was in the bag! Meddle carefully took it out and looked at it. It was a thin silver wand, and it felt strangely heavy in his hands.

Meddle was suddenly full of excitement. He would use the wand and see if he could make it do some magic for him! So he waved it in the air and wished!

"I wish for a sack of gold!"

There was a thud beside him—and a great brown sack appeared, tied up at the neck. Meddle trembled with joy. Oooh! The wand was really magic. Look at this enormous sack!

"I must hide it outside where no one will see it!" said Meddle. So he dragged it outside and hid it behind the wall. Then he crept into the little room again and picked up the silver wand.

"What shall I wish for this time?" he wondered. He looked down at his shoes, and saw that they were very muddy from going out into the garden. That would never do! So Meddle waved the wand and wished

once more.

"I wish for a beautiful pair of golden shoes on my feet!" Something flew off his feet—and his old shoes were gone! Something clapped themselves *on* his feet—and bless us all, there was Meddle wearing the most beautiful pair of real gold shoes, shining and glittering like the sun!

"Gracious!" said Meddle. "I *am* getting on! I'll wish for something else now, before the conjurer comes back. I can hear him talking to Mrs. Twinkle.

"I wish for my larder at home to be filled with all sorts of things to eat—treacle puddings, jam rolls, chocolate cakes, ice-creams, and anything else that's nice!" he wished. Then he heard the conjurer coming and he slipped out of the room and ran to where the others were still playing Nuts in May.

Now, when the conjurer was standing in front of everyone, later on, looking at all the guests sitting in their chairs, he picked up his magic wand to do some magic. And as soon as he picked it up and waved it, he

26

knew someone had been meddling with it!

How did he know? Oh, quite easily! You see, when a wand is full of magic, it is very heavy—but it gets lighter as it is used. And Meddle had used it three times, so that now it was very light indeed.

The conjurer looked in astonishment at his wand. Then he glared at all the people in front of him.

"Someone," he said, "SOMEONE has been using my wand. The goodness is gone out of it. *Who* has done this?"

Nobody answered. Meddle was dreadfully frightened. He hadn't guessed that the conjurer would find out. How he wished he hadn't meddled with the magic wand now!

"I say again," said the conjurer, in a very angry voice, "*WHO* has used my wand? I will give them this one chance—and I warn them that if they do not come forward and tell me, they will be punished, and will be very sorry indeed."

Meddle sat quite still in his chair. *He* wasn't going to own up. Not he! How could the conjurer punish him if he didn't know who it was that had used the wand?

"Very well," said the conjurer. "I will say no more. But the one who has used my magic will be very sorry before the night has gone."

The party went on. Mister Meddle didn't enjoy it a bit, because he knew he should not have touched the wand, and he knew that he certainly should have owned up when the conjurer had spoken about it.

All the same, he was delighted to think he had a sack of gold, golden shoes on his feet, and a cupboard full of the most delicious food at home!

When the time came to say good-bye, Meddle slipped away first, dragging with him on his shoulder

his enormous sack. He went down the darkest lanes so that he should not meet anyone.

The sack was terribly heavy. He had to keep putting it down and resting. Really, he had never known such a heavy sack in all his life! He would be very rich with all that gold!

Suddenly his feet began to hurt him. His golden shoes were heavy and tight, and they began to press on his toes and heels in a very painful manner.

"I'll take them off and put them in my pocket," thought Mister Meddle. "Then they won't hurt me. I can easily walk in my stockinged feet."

But he couldn't get the golden

shoes off! They just simply would *not* come off! He tried and he tried, but it was no use at all.

So there was nothing for it but to go on wearing them, though poor Meddle groaned and grunted at every step! At last he got home. He dragged the sack into his kitchen and lighted his lamp. He took a knife and cut the string that bound up the neck of the sack.

He put in his hand to get out the gold—but oh, what a dreadful, dreadful disappointment! The sack was full of nothing but big stones! The magic had gone out of it and the gold had turned to nasty, heavy stones. Poor Meddle—he had dragged stones all the way home!

He sat down to take off his shoes,

which were hurting him more than ever. But no—it was impossible to take them off. Meddle began to feel frightened. The gold had turned to stones—and the shoes wouldn't come off! He didn't like it at all!

"Never mind—perhaps I'll find all those delicious things in my cupboard that I wished for," he thought. "I'm hungry now—I'll have a few!"

He went to the cupboard and opened it, half afraid that he wouldn't find anything there. But on the shelves were the treacle puddings, the chocolate cakes, the jam rolls, and many other things he had wished for. Good!

He took down an ice-cream and fetched a spoon. He put a spoonful

into his mouth—but, good gracious me, he spat it out again at once! It burnt his tongue! Yes, it really did! Meddle stared at the ice-cream as if he couldn't believe his eyes. How could ice burn? He must have been mistaken. He tried again. But this time the ice-cream burnt his tongue so much that he screamed and ran to get some cold water.

Then he tried the treacle pudding — but the treacle tasted like salt and was horrible. He bit a chocolate biscuit, but it tasted of cardboard and he couldn't swallow it. He licked the jam off a tart, but it was made of pepper and made him sneeze and choke till the tears came into his eyes!

"Oh, it's too bad, it's too bad!" said Meddle, in despair. "All the magic has gone wrong. Why didn't I own up when I had the chance? Here I've tired myself out dragging a heavy sack of stones all the way home — and my feet are almost crippled with these dreadfully tight shoes — and now I've burnt my tongue, and tasted all sorts of horrible things that look as nice as can be!"

He decided to go to bed—but still he couldn't get his shoes off, and they seemed to be growing tighter and tighter and tighter. It was dreadful!

At last, in despair, Mister Meddle went out into the dark night with his lantern, to go back to Mrs. Twinkle's and ask if the conjurer was still there. He really, really must get these shoes off his feet! He would have to confess—and say he was sorry. He really *was* sorry, too. It was a dreadful thing to meddle with someone else's magic.

The conjurer was staying the night at Mrs. Twinkle's. He didn't seem a bit surprised to see the trembling Meddle. He stared at him without a smile.

"I was expecting you," he said sternly. "Meddlers are always punished."

"Please forgive me," begged Meddle. "My sack of gold turned to stones.

My larder of good things cannot be eaten — and my feet are so tired of these shoes."

"You must wear them for three days," said the conjurer, looking at them. "I cannot take them off, for the magic is too strong. As for the things in your larder, throw them away, for they will be of no use to anyone."

Poor Meddle! He limped home, crying. He threw away all the lovely things in his larder, and he emptied his sack of stones at the bottom of the garden. Then he went to bed with his golden shoes on!

And for three days he had to wear them. Then they became looser and he took them off and threw them down the well. Horrible things! He wasn't going to keep them!

"That's taught me never to meddle again!" said Mister Meddle solemnly. "Never — never — never!"

And he didn't meddle with anything for a whole month. But after that — well, I'm afraid he forgot again. That's another story!

CHAPTER III

MISTER MEDDLE AT THE STATION

It happened once that Mister Meddle went to the railway station to see his old friends Pippin and his wife off by train.

Now Pippin wasn't at all pleased to see Meddle, for he knew what muddles people got into when Meddle was anywhere about! So he just nodded to Meddle, and tried to pretend that he was far too busy to bother with him.

"Pippin!" cried Meddle. "Are you very busy?"

"Very," said Pippin. "I've lots of things to do—tickets to get—luggage to see to—the right train to find—haven't a minute to spare, Meddle. Good-bye!"

"My dear old friend, if you're as busy as all that, I must really help you!" cried Meddle. "Now—let me get the tickets for you! Where are you going to?"

"We're going to Lemon Village," said Pippin. "But I can get the tickets. Don't you bother, Meddle."

"No bother, no bother at all!" cried Mister Meddle. He held out his hand for the money and Pippin gave him some.

"I want a ticket for my parrot too," he said. "I've got it in a cage here." Meddle rushed off. There were a lot of people by the ticket-office waiting their turn to get tickets. Meddle took up his place and waited. At last he got to the ticket-man.

"Where to?" asked the man impatiently. Mister Meddle frowned. Now where did Pippin say he and his wife were going to?

"Er — er — two tickets for Orange Town, and an extra ticket for a

canary," said Meddle at last. He paid for the tickets and rushed back. On the way he thought he would try and find out what platform the train left from.

"Where's the train for Orange Town?" asked Meddle when a porter passed.

"Number eight platform, and the train leaves at five minutes past eleven!" said the porter.

"Good gracious!" cried Meddle in alarm. "Why, Pippin said it left at a *quarter* past eleven—he'll miss it! I wonder whether he has got his luggage there yet."

Meddle looked round, and nearby he saw a pile of luggage, with a canary's cage set on top. "That must be their luggage!" he cried. "Good!

I'll see to it for them! Hie, porter!"

A porter hurried up. "Take this luggage to platform number eight, and put it on the five-past-eleven train to Orange Town," said Meddle, in a grand voice. He did love seeing to things.

The porter stared. "But a lady told me to leave it here just now whilst she went to get a cup of tea," he said.

"My good man, do as you're told!" said Meddle. "Look—here are the tickets—one for the canary too—now just do as you are told!"

The porter put the things on his barrow, for he thought that if Meddle had the tickets he must own the luggage. Off he trundled to the train on platform number eight, and put the things neatly into a carriage.

Meddle looked about for his friends. They would certainly miss the train if they didn't hurry! He would buy them some chocolate to eat on the train. That was a good idea. So he ran to a machine, put in two pennies —and got out two boxes of matches, which he felt quite sure were chocolate! Really, Meddle!

He still couldn't see Pippin and Mrs. Pippin. And then at last he caught sight of them in the carriage of a train nearby! "You're in the wrong train!" shouted Meddle. "Hie, Pippin, your train is on platform eight!"

Pippin looked alarmed. He jumped out of the carriage and helped Mrs. Pippin out too. He called to a porter to bring their things from the

carriage and ran to Pippin.

"Are you sure?" he said. "We did ask if this was right and we were told it was."

"You leave things to me," said Meddle, importantly. "I've arranged everything. I've got your tickets for you—and some chocolate. Come along at once."

Meddle hurried Mr. and Mrs. Pippin to platform eight. It was almost time for that train to go. He found the carriage where the luggage and the canary cage were, and put Pippin and his wife in. Behind them hurried the porter with their things from the other train, a big parrot cage on top.

"But this looks as if somebody else had taken this carriage," said Pippin, looking round at the luggage already there, and the canary's cage on the rack above their heads.

"Here is some chocolate for you both," said Meddle, and he pushed the boxes of matches into Pippin's hand. Pippin looked at the matches.

"Are you quite mad, Meddle?" he said. "These are matches! We can't eat those?"

"Oh dear!" said Meddle – and then he suddenly caught sight of the porter with all the luggage belonging to the Pippins. The man pushed Meddle aside and began to put the luggage into the carriage.

"My good man, this carriage is already full of people and luggage," said Meddle grandly. "Take it away."

"But, Meddle, that's *our* luggage," said Mrs. Pippin, who was getting very tired of Meddle. "Of course the man must put it in. We don't want to leave it behind!"

"*Your* luggage!" said Meddle, in a surprised voice. "But I don't understand. Surely all this is yours that I got the other porter to put here – and see, there's your canary cage!"

"Canary cage!" snorted Pippin.

"Don't be silly, Meddle. We haven't any canary. We've a parrot. Look out —here comes the cage. Mind the parrot doesn't peck you!"

The parrot put its curved beak through the bars of its cage and tweaked Meddle's arm. He yelled.

"Don't! Oh, I say, Pippin, this is very strange. All the other luggage that I told the other porter to put in here must belong to somebody else then! Oh dear!"

The engine whistled. A ticket-collector came. "Can I see your tickets, please?" he asked. "The train is just going."

Meddle gave Pippin the tickets he had bought and Pippin showed them to the collector. "Orange Town!" said the man. "Change at Holly

Corner."

"But we're not going to Orange Town, we're going to Lemon Village!" cried Pippin in alarm.

"Not in this train," said the collector. "It goes the other way! The Lemon Village train starts from

49

platform number two in ten minutes' time. Hop out quickly!"

Pippin and Mrs. Pippin hopped out and threw their luggage on to the platform. They took the parrot from the rack just in time, for the train shook itself and then steamed off to Holly Corner! All the other luggage, canary and all, went off in the empty carriage.

"Go away, Meddle!" shouted Pippin angrily. "Go away! You've made enough muddles to last us for a month! I shall change the tickets, and find my own train again. Taking tickets to Orange Town indeed, when we wanted Lemon Village — and buying a canary's ticket when we wanted a parrot's! Here, take your matches — *we* don't want them!"

Biff-smack! The two boxes hit Meddle on the nose. Then Pippin and his wife hurried to platform number two with their luggage, and Pippin sent the porter to change the tickets. There was just time!

Meddle felt very hurt. He thought he had better vanish away—but what

was this? A porter came up to him with a large, fierce-looking lady.

"Here's the fellow that told me to put your luggage and your canary into the train for Orange Town," said the porter. "They've gone now, Madam."

"Oh, they have, have they?" said the large fierce lady, and she took Mister Meddle by his long nose. "I suppose you are one of these meddling, interfering people who just make trouble for everybody! Well, you come along with me and we'll see what the station-master has to say to you!"

The station-master said a lot, and in the end Mister Meddle had to buy himself a ticket to Orange Town and go and fetch the luggage and the canary he had sent there. He felt very upset indeed.

"I'll never bother to help any one again!" he vowed. "I really—really—won't!"

But he just can't keep that long nose of his out of other people's business!

CHAPTER IV

MISTER MEDDLE GOES OUT TO TEA

Once Mister Meddle went out to tea with Sally Simple. Sally didn't know Meddle as well as most people did, or she might not have asked him.

He arrived at Sally's house dressed in his best. He was early, and Sally Simple was not quite ready.

"Oh, never mind, never mind!" said Meddle, beaming. "Just give me a few jobs to do for you about the house, dear Sally, and I'll be quite happy. I love helping people."

Sally Simple thought what a nice fellow Mister Meddle was. "Well," she said, "you might feed the goldfish

54

for me, if you will, and you might
put some more food into the canary's
cage."

"Certainly, certainly!" said Meddle.
"Anything else? Those jobs won't
take me long."

"Well—would you put the kettle on
to boil?" asked Sally. "And would
you like to go and pick some ripe

strawberries for tea? They are lovely just now."

"I'd love to!" said Meddle, rubbing his hands in delight. "Strawberries! Ha! Just what I like. Have you any cream?"

"There's a jar of cream in the larder," said Sally. "Now, I'll just go upstairs and put on a clean blouse. I won't be long. You'll find the bird-seed and the goldfish food in the cup-board over there."

Sally ran upstairs, thinking it was a real pleasure to meet anyone so friendly and helpful as Mister Meddle.

Meddle looked at the two goldfish swimming in their little bowl. He looked at the canary. "I'll give you your dinner!" he said. "Pretty things, pretty things!"

"Tweet!" said the canary, but the goldfish said nothing at all.

Meddle went to the cupboard. There were two packets there—one of goldfish food, which was ants' eggs, or rather ant-grub cocoons, and the other was canary-seed.

What did silly old Meddle do but scatter bird-seed on the top of the goldfish bowl, and give the ants' eggs to the canary! The canary put its head on one side and pecked up the eggs. It liked them. But the goldfish didn't like the bird-seed at all.

"Not hungry, I suppose," said Meddle, watching the goldfish swimming about. "You haven't snapped at a single bit of your food, fish! Now, what else was I to do? Oh—put the kettle on to boil, of course!"

Meddle took up the kettle and set it on the stove. He didn't think of filling it with water. He just put it there to boil — without water!

"Now for the strawberries!" he said. He took a basket and went out into the garden. There were heaps of lovely red strawberries. It didn't take Meddle long to fill his basket. He went back to the house, whistling merrily.

He put the strawberries on a chair, and went to look for the cream. There was a jar in the cupboard full of yellow cream. Meddle emptied some into a jug and set it on the table. He didn't know that it was furniture cream that he had taken out of the polish-jar! No — Meddle never thought of things like that!

Sally Simple came down looking very nice. She beamed at Meddle. "Done all your jobs?" she asked.

"Yes," said Meddle. "I've fed the goldfish—look!"

Sally looked, and then she looked again. "Do you usually feed gold-fish with bird-seed?" she said, in

rather an annoyed voice. "Why did you do that, Mister Meddle? I suppose you thought it would make them sing."

Meddle went red. He looked at the canary's cage, and so did Sally. "And you've given the canary the ants' eggs," she said. "Well, well, Meddle, I did think you knew the difference between goldfish and canaries, but if you don't I suppose you just can't help it!"

"I *do* know the difference!" said Meddle.

"I shouldn't have thought you did then," said Sally. "Now, is the kettle boiling? It doesn't look as if it is — no steam is coming from its spout!"

"I put it on ages ago," said Meddle.

Sally took it up from the stove. It

felt very light indeed. Sally glared at Meddle. "There's no water in it!" she cried. "Did you expect a kettle to boil without water?"

"Er — no," said Meddle, feeling very foolish.

"Oh, look! The kettle has got a hole burnt in the bottom now — all because you were silly enough to put it on without water in!" cried Sally crossly. "What will you do next?"

"I'm very sorry," said Meddle, and he sat down on a chair, feeling rather upset. And, of course, he chose the chair on which he had put the basket of strawberries! Squish, squash!

"That's right, Meddle—strawberries are meant to be sat on, not eaten!" said Sally scornfully. "I suppose that's what you put them there for—to sit on!"

"They're all right," said Meddle, getting up and looking at the squashed basket and strawberries. "Just a bit flattened, that's all. We will be able to eat them all right."

"Well, if you want to eat sat-on strawberries, you can," said Sally.

"But I'm not going to. Did you find the cream? Or did you put out marmalade or something instead?"

"If you look in the jug, you'll see I put out cream," said Meddle, very much hurt. Sally looked into the jug. The cream looked a bit yellow to her. She smelt it—and she knew that Meddle had put out the furniture cream instead of the real cream. She smiled a little smile to herself.

"You are sure this cream will be all right with sat-on strawberries?" she asked.

"Perfectly all right," said Meddle. He emptied the squashed strawberries on to a plate and poured the cream all over them. He scattered sugar on them too. Then he took up a spoon and began to eat.

He didn't like the first mouthful at all. Oh dear, what a dreadful taste! He took another—but no, he really couldn't eat it!

"I feel ill, Sally," he said in a faint voice. "I think I'll go home. Goodbye! I'll come to tea with you another day."

"You may not be asked!" said Sally, and she shut the door behind Meddle.

Poor Mister Meddle! He didn't eat strawberries-and-cream again for a long time!

CHAPTER V

MISTER MEDDLE ON THE FARM

Did you ever hear how Mister Meddle went to visit his sister, the farmer's wife? It's a funny story, to be sure!

Dame Henny wasn't at all pleased to see Meddle. She knew what a dreadful fellow he was for getting into a fix. But as he was her brother she had to make him welcome.

"You've come on rather a busy day for me," said Dame Henny. "It's baking day, you see, so I'm afraid I shan't have much time to spare you, Meddle."

"Oh, don't worry about that," said Meddle. "I'll help you. I can go and collect the eggs — and milk the cows — and feed the pigs — and . . ."

"Meddle, I'd rather you didn't do a single *thing*!" said Dame Henny at once. "You're no good on a farm at all. I don't believe you know the difference between a hen and a duck!"

Meddle was offended. He sat down and ate a piece of cake and drank a glass of milk without saying a word. Dame Henny hoped that he was so offended he would go home. But he didn't.

"I'll just show my silly sister that I know a lot more than she thinks," he said to himself. "I'll just show her!"

So out he went to look for eggs. But Dame Henny had already hunted in all the nests and had taken every one. However, in two coops by themselves were two hens sitting on twelve eggs each, hatching them into chicks.

Meddle didn't know they were hatching the eggs. He thought they had laid them all. "Ha!" he said, pleased. "Look at that! Twelve eggs in *this* nest that my sister hasn't

seen — and, dear me, twelve in this one! Oh! You bad hen, you! You pecked my hand so hard that you've made it bleed!"

Meddle collected all the twenty-four eggs into a big basket. The hens screeched and pecked at him, for they were upset to see their precious eggs taken. But Meddle proudly took them back to Dame Henny.

"Look here!" he said, showing her the eggs. "Twenty-four eggs you missed this morning! What do you think of that? It's a good thing I came."

"Meddle!" said Dame Henny in amazement. "Where in the world did you find them? Has one of the hens been laying away?"

"Oh no," said Meddle. "I found

twelve eggs in one coop with a silly pecking hen on them, and twelve eggs in another."

"Oh, you silly, stupid, meddling creature!" cried Dame Henny in a rage. "Those are the eggs that the two hens are hatching into chicks for me. You may have spoilt them! Give them to me! I must take them back at once."

Dame Henny snatched the eggs away from Meddle and ran off to put them back into the coops. Meddle was cross. He went out and looked at the pigs.

"My! How hungry they are!" he said, as he watched them rooting about in their sty. "I don't believe my sister gives them enough to eat."

He rushed indoors. On the table was

a big bowl full of some sort of mixture. Meddle took it and ran to the pigs.

"This must be meant for you," he said, as he put the bowl down for the pigs to eat from. "It looks like what they call pig-wash."

The pigs ran to the big bowl and began to gobble up the mixture there with joy. Dame Henny came back from the coops and stared into the sty. When she saw her basin there she glared at Meddle.

"Where did you get that basin, and what's in it?" she asked.

"I don't exactly know what the mixture is," said Meddle. "I found the bowl on your kitchen table, and as the pigs were hungry I thought I'd better give them their dinner."

"On my kitchen table!" shouted Dame Henny in a fine temper. "Why, that was my mixing-bowl—and in it was my cake-mixture! There were eggs and flour and milk and currants and sugar in that bowl—and you've given it all to the greedy pigs! Oh, you wicked fellow! I'll box your ears for you, so I will!"

Meddle ran away and hid inside a shed. He didn't like his ears boxed. Dame Henny snorted angrily and went indoors. She had some buns baking in the oven and she didn't want them to be burnt.

Meddle looked round the dark shed. At first he thought he was alone, but then he saw a big animal at the far end.

"It's a cow!" said Meddle in surprise. "Now why isn't the poor thing out in the field with the others? It must have been forgotten! Really, how careless people are! I will let the poor thing out into the air and sunshine."

He went to where the big animal chewed quietly in its corner. It was tied with a heavy rope to its stall.

Meddle undid the rope.

"Gee up!" he said, and the great creature lumbered out. It was pleased to be free and in the sunshine. It bellowed loudly.

"Gee up, I say!" said Meddle, and he swished the back legs of the animal with a twig. It bellowed again.

Dame Henny heard the bellowing and came running to the kitchen door. She gave a scream.

"Who's let out the bull?" she cried. "Oh my, oh my, now what are we to do? Who's let out the bull? Help, help, the bull is loose!"

"Oh, is it a bull?" cried Meddle in alarm. "I thought it was just a cow. It was standing all alone in the dark shed and I thought somebody had forgotten it."

The bull bellowed again and swished its long tail about. Its eyes gleamed fiercely as it looked at Meddle. It had not liked being hit with a stinging twig on its back legs.

"Meddle, you got that bull out—now you just take it back again!" cried Dame Henny.

"Well, it seems a harmless creature," said Meddle. "Bellows a bit, that's all! Hie, you bull! Go back to your shed! Do you hear? Pretending to be a lonely cow like that, and making me set you free! I never heard of such a thing! Go back to your shed at once!"

But the bull didn't mean to go back to the dark shed. It kicked up its heels and frisked round the farmyard, trying to find a way into the buttercup-field where the cows and the sheep grazed quietly.

Meddle was angry. "Didn't you hear what I said, you bad creature?" he cried. "I'll whip you with my switch! There! How do you like that?"

The bull felt the stick against his

back legs and he didn't like it at all. He turned and glared at Meddle. Then he lowered his head and began to run towards Meddle.

"Run, Meddle, run! He'll toss you on his horns!" shouted Dame Henny.

"Stop, bull, stop!" called Meddle in alarm. "I'll open the gate into the field for you. Stop! Don't be silly! I'm your friend!"

"Brrrrrrrrumph!" snorted the angry bull and rushed straight at Meddle. Meddle ran to the gate—but the bull caught him up. He tore two holes in Meddle's trousers and tossed him up into the air, right over the hedge—and, dear me, Meddle fell neatly on to a cow's back, smack!

The cow was in a fright when she felt Meddle on her back. She tore

round the field with Meddle clinging to her horns—and at that moment Farmer Henny came back home from market.

When he saw Meddle on a cow he was very angry, for he thought that someone was having a joke with his cows. He waited till the cow threw Meddle off, and then he stepped up to him with his big stick.

"People that ride cows get a whipping!" he said. "Smack! Thud!"

"Oh! Oh! Stop!" cried Meddle. "I'm Meddle, your wife's brother. Don't you know me?"

"Oh yes, I know you all right!" said the farmer, grinning. "That's why I'm going on. Smack! Thud!"

Meddle took to his heels and ran off like the wind. Farmer Henny laughed.

"I'll never visit you again!" shouted Meddle in a rage. "Never, never, never!"

"That suits us all right!" cried the farmer, and he went to catch his bull.

As for Mister Meddle, he had to spend the next day in bed whilst Mrs. Stitch mended his trousers!

CHAPTER VI

MISTER MEDDLE GOES TO THE GROCER'S

One morning Mister Meddle took his shopping-basket and went to the grocer's. He wanted a dozen eggs. They were a penny each, he knew, so he slipped a shilling into his pocket to pay for them.

When he got there, Mr. Sugarman, the grocer, was not in his usual place behind the counter. He had gone out to his yard to get some oil for a customer. Mister Meddle wandered round the shop, looking at the biscuits and bacon and eggs.

Dame Flap came in and said good morning. She sat down on a chair and waited.

"I can't think what's happened to Mr. Sugarman," said Mister Meddle. "I've been waiting quite a time."

"It's a nuisance," said Dame Flap. "I'm in a hurry. I want some castor sugar to put on the top of a nice jam-sandwich."

"Well, I'll get it for you," said Mister Meddle, most obligingly. "You can leave the money on the counter for Mr. Sugarman when he comes in, and I'll tell him it's for a pound of sugar."

He hunted about for castor sugar. At last he found a big tin-lined drawer of what he thought was sugar — but, you know, it was salt! Mister Meddle didn't think of tasting to make sure. No — he simply weighed out a pound, put it into Dame Flap's bag, and she put the money on the counter.

"It's nice to be useful," thought Mister Meddle, sitting down to wait. As he waited, the door-bell rang and old Father Jenks came in.

"Hallo, where's Mr. Sugarman?" he asked. "I want some caraway seeds. My wife is baking a seed-cake, and she's got no caraway seeds."

"Let me serve you, Father Jenks!" said Mister Meddle, jumping up. "I'll soon find the seeds for you!"

He hunted around, and came to a big tin of seeds. "These must be caraway seeds," said Meddle, pleased. If only he had looked on the outside of the tin he would have seen that it was full of canary seed—but no, Mister Meddle didn't think of looking. He was quite sure it was full of caraway seeds.

He weighed out a little packet of them and gave them to Father Jenks. "I don't know how much caraway seeds are, but if you leave a shilling Mr. Sugarman will send you the change," said Mister Meddle grandly.

So Father Jenks put a shilling on the counter, took up the packet, and

went out. Mister Meddle really felt he was being remarkably useful. He hoped somebody else would come in — and sure enough, somebody did!

It was little Molly Miggle. She wanted some butter. Mister Meddle beamed at her.

He saw some yellow tablets on a shelf that looked to him just like butter. He took one down and wrapped it up. He didn't see that it was yellow soap. Silly old Meddle!

Molly Miggle put down ninepence on the counter and went out. Mister Meddle was just going to sit down when Spink came in to do some shopping. Spink was a sharp little fellow who didn't like Meddle at all.

"What can I do for you this morning, Spink?" said Meddle.

"Do for me? What do you mean?" said Spink. "You're not the grocer!"

"Oh, I'm just serving people till Mr. Sugarman comes back," said Meddle. "Do tell me what you want."

"Well, I shan't," said Spink. "I'm quite able to get what I want myself. I know you and your meddling ways."

Mister Meddle felt angry. Spink walked over to the eggs and picked out one or two, weighing them in his hand to get the heaviest ones.

Meddle went and stood at his elbow. "You are not to do that," he said to Spink. "It's not fair to take the best eggs. You should take them as they come."

"Oh, go away," said Spink, giving Meddle a sharp dig with his elbow. Meddle gave a squeal, and then dug *his* elbow into Spink. Spink shouted and turned on Meddle. He gave him a good shaking and then let go of him suddenly. Meddle fell straight into the box of new-laid eggs!

Crash! Smash! He broke about a hundred eggs at one go! He sat up in the box, covered with yellow yolk, very angry indeed. Spink yelled with laughter and danced round the shop in delight. "You can pay for them!" he shouted. "You can pay for them!"

He ran out of the shop, still laughing. Meddle was just struggling to get out of the egg-box when Mr. Sugarman the grocer came in. He stared at Meddle in the greatest astonishment. "Are you trying to hatch those eggs?" he asked at last. "I'm afraid it will be expensive, Mister Meddle."

"Spink pushed me in," said Meddle, trying to get out. "You must make him pay for them, Mr. Sugarman. I was only trying to stop him taking your nicest eggs. And I've been very helpful to you this morning, if only you knew it! I've served heaps of customers!"

And at that moment the three

customers all came into the shop together, very angry indeed. Dame Flap slapped a blue bag down on the counter and glared at Meddle.

"You gave me salt instead of sugar!" she cried angrily. "You muddler! You meddler! I've spoilt my sandwich! It's got salt all over it now instead of sugar!"

"And just look here — my wife says you gave me canary seed instead of caraway seed!" shouted Father Jenks in a rage. "She emptied half of it into her cake mixture before she saw it was the wrong seed — and now I've got to spend the rest of the morning picking out those seeds! I've a good mind to pull your nose hard! Sticking it into other people's business like that!"

"And my mother says this is yellow soap, not butter," said Molly Miggle, putting the soap on the counter. "She tried to cut it to spread on our bread, and it wouldn't spread—and when she tasted a bit she found it was soap, and it made her feel ill. She's very angry indeed."

Mr. Sugarman glared at Meddle.

"Can't you stop meddling with other people?" he said. "I shall send you in a bill for canary seed, soap, and salt, my dear Meddle. And I should like to know what *you* came to buy this morning? A pennyworth of sense, I should think."

"I came to buy some eggs," said Meddle, getting out of the egg-box, looking very hot and bothered to hear of all his mistakes.

"Well, you seem to have got your eggs all right," said Dame Flap, giggling as she saw Meddle covered with yolks.

"Put a few into your basket," said Mr. Sugarman, and he shook the mess of broken eggs into Meddle's basket. "I'll send in the bill to-morrow. Good-day!"

Poor Meddle! He had to walk all the way home covered in egg-yolk, and he didn't like it at all.

"Have you sat down in a custard?" yelled the boys and girls he passed. Mister Meddle didn't say a word. He went indoors and put himself and his clothes into a nice hot bath.

And whilst he was steaming there, he made up his mind as usual that he wouldn't meddle any more.

Dear, dear! What a pity he can't do what he says!

CHAPTER VII

MISTER MEDDLE'S PARCEL

One day Mister Meddle went to get his shoes from the cobbler's. They were ready for him, so he paid the bill and took up the brown paper parcel.

Off he went, meaning to go straight home. But, of course, he didn't. He met Mr. Jenks, who was sitting on the seat by the bus-stop with a lot of other people, waiting for the bus.

So down sat Meddle and began to talk. Mr. Jenks caught the next bus, and then, as Meddle didn't know any of the other people on the seat, he picked up the parcel beside him and set off home.

But he had picked up the wrong

parcel! He had put his parcel down on the left side of him — and the one he picked up was on the right side, and belonged to the big man there! But the big man didn't notice for a while. He just sat and smoked his pipe.

Meddle went on home, swinging his

parcel by the string and singing a
song at the top of his voice. But he
hadn't gone very far when he heard
someone shouting behind him.

He looked round. It was the big
man, and he was shouting out very
loudly:

"GIVE ME THAT PARCEL!"

"Good gracious!" said Meddle to
himself, quite alarmed. "What does
he want my parcel for? He must be
a robber!"

So Meddle began to run as fast
as he could.

"STOP! STOP!" yelled the big
man behind. "I SAY STOP!"

"And I say go on!" panted Meddle
to himself. "Oh my, oh my! Who'd
have thought of meeting robbers like
this!"

He tore on and on. The man tore after him, getting angrier and angrier.

"GIVE ME THAT PARCEL!" yelled the man, who was really catching Meddle up now.

"Never, never!" shouted back Meddle valiantly. He turned in at a gate, meaning to take a short cut across Farmer Straw's field. It was very muddy and wet. Soon poor Meddle had lumps of clay on his boots, and could hardly run at all. He staggered as he went—but the big man behind was in the same state!

He couldn't run either, for his boots had great lumps of clay all over them. But he made up for his slowness by his shouting.

"STOP, I SAY! STOP! I WANT THAT PARCEL!"

"Well, you won't get it then!" shouted back poor Meddle. He stumbled over the field and at last came to the stream. This was usually so small that Meddle could jump over it quite easily. But to-day it was swollen and wide and deep, for there had been heavy rains. Meddle wished he hadn't got to jump—but there was nothing else to do!

So he jumped—but, of course, he landed right in the very middle of the stream! His parcel got very wet, and by the time he had waded out of the stream on to the other side, the paper was giving way. Meddle sat down on the bank, panting and puffing. He felt quite sure that the big man wouldn't try to jump, for he had seen what had happened to Meddle.

The man didn't jump. He stood on the other side of the stream and shouted once more to him:

"You SILLY! You've spoilt my parcel!"

Meddle thought the man must be quite mad. He held up the parcel, which was rapidly coming undone, and shouted back:

"It's *my* parcel! It's got my boots inside! You won't rob me of them if I can help it."

The paper slid away, and big drops of water fell all over Meddle. He stared at the wet paper—and he stared, and he stared! For in the parcel were not the boots he had expected—but a very nice large slab of cheese that smelt exceedingly good—but was quite spoilt by the water!"

"Good gracious!" said Meddle. "What's happened to my boots?"

"You left them on the bus-stop seat, you silly donkey," said the big man impatiently. "You took my cheese instead. And here I've been

shouting and running after you for ages, and all you do is to yell back something rude at me, jump into a stream, and spoil my cheese!"

"I'm really very sorry," said Meddle in a small voice. "Really very sorry indeed."

"Well, being sorry won't mend

99

my cheese," said the big man. "You'll have to pay for that."

"Oh, certainly," said Meddle. "I quite see that. I'll send the money to you to-morrow."

"Oh no, you won't," said the big man firmly. "You'll come across this stream again and you'll give me the money now. After all, you've got to go back to the seat to fetch your boots, haven't you? And you'd better hurry, too, in case somebody goes off with them!"

"Dear me, so I had," said poor Meddle. So into the stream he had to jump once more. He waded across and paid the large man what he asked. Then, cramming the soaked cheese into his pocket, he set off back to the seat to get his boots.

The parcel was still there. Meddle undid it to make sure it really did hold boots this time, not cheese or something extraordinary. Yes—it was boots all right!

So home at last went Meddle, with a pair of mended boots, a pocketful of dripping cheese—and no money!

And if I know anything of Meddle, he'll go to bed to-night, leaving the cheese in his pockets—and then he'll wonder why his bedroom is suddenly overrun with hundreds of mice!

CHAPTER VIII

MISTER MEDDLE AND THE BIRDS

One day when Mister Meddle passed by his Aunt Jemima's, he saw that she had some new yellow canaries and some little budgie-birds, too.

"Dear me!" said Meddle in delight. "How pretty they are! I really must go and see them!"

He popped into his aunt's house, and she came running to send him out, for she knew Meddle's interfering ways.

"Now, Meddle, out you go!" she said. "It's my washing morning and I can't have you around upsetting things and making muddles."

"Aunt Jemima, I only came in to

see your lovely new birds," said
Meddle crossly. "Just let me look at
them, now do!"

"Well, take one look and go!"
said his aunt. Meddle peered into
the big canary-cage. There were two
fine canaries there, tweeting loudly.
The budgies were flying free around

the room, calling to one another. They had a little perch by the window and they often flew to this to look out and see the passers-by.

"Aunt Jemima, your birds haven't very much to eat," said Meddle. "Look—only just that bit of seed—and very nasty dry stuff it looks too! Why don't you feed them properly?"

"I do," said his aunt, vexed. "You don't know anything about birds, Meddle, so don't pretend you do!"

"Oh, Aunt Jemima, I know a GREAT DEAL!" said Meddle. "Birds eat worms and caterpillars and flies and grubs—they love those. Look at that canary tweeting at me with its head on one side. It knows I understand it."

"Well, you go and do a little

understanding outside," said his aunt, giving him a push. "*I* know somebody who gave fish-food to Sally Simple's canary—and gave her canary seed to goldfish. Ha, ha, that's all you know about birds."

Meddle was really very angry indeed. He walked outside in a huff without even saying good morning. But, as he went, he made up his mind to do something for his aunt's canaries and budgies.

"Poor things! Only that dry seed to eat!" he said. "I'll collect some worms and caterpillars for them. If they were flying about like the thrushes and the blackbirds, that's what they would be feeding on! I'll take them to the birds when Aunt Jemima is out."

So Meddle began to hunt about his garden for worms and caterpillars. He had a bag for the worms and a box for the caterpillars—and, dear me, what a lot he found! He found a few beetles too, and wondered if the birds would like those as well. He put them into a tin.

Then he waited for Tuesday afternoon when he knew Aunt Jemima went out to a sewing-meeting. He put all the things into his pocket and set off, thinking happily how pleased the birds would be to have a good meal. He crept into the kitchen of Aunt Jemima's house. Not a sound was to be heard.

"Good! She's gone already!" said Meddle, full of delight. He took out his bag of worms, his box of

caterpillars, and his tin of beetles. He tiptoed into the front room.

The worms were very wriggly. Meddle found it difficult to push them through the bars of the cage. The poor worms didn't like it at all. So Meddle decided to give them to the budgies—but they were frightened of him and wouldn't come for the worms. They flew all over the room, perching on the lamp, the pictures, and the curtains.

"Oh, very well, you silly things," said Meddle crossly. "After I've taken all this trouble you might at least be pleased to see me. Well, I'll hang the worms here and there and you can get them when you like."

So Meddle draped the worms about the room — two or three on the lamp-shade, some on the top of the pic-tures, and one or two on the mantel-piece. Then he opened his box of caterpillars. They were very lively indeed.

"I'm not sure it wouldn't be a good idea to let the canaries out of their cage and give them a fly round the room," said Meddle. "After all,

the budgies are loose. Then I can pop
the caterpillars and grubs here and
there, and all the birds can share
them. It will be as much fun for
them as flying round my garden to
find them."

It wasn't much fun for the caterpillars and worms! But Meddle didn't

think of that. He put the caterpillars on the table and chairs and pictures, and he popped the beetles on the mantelpiece, where they immediately ran to hide themselves away.

The canaries were rather frightened when they were let out of their cage. They took no notice of the live food that Meddle had brought. The budgies didn't seem to want it either. Meddle was disgusted with them.

"Well, really, you might . . ." he began. And then he stopped and listened in a dreadful fright.

Aunt Jemima was coming in at the front door, and with her were five friends! This Tuesday was Aunt Jemima's turn for having the sewing-meeting at her own house.

Meddle got a terrible scare. There

wasn't time for him to escape. He hurriedly squeezed himself between the sofa and the wall and hid there. He did hope that the six women would not come in that room.

But they did! In they trooped all chattering merrily, and sat down. They put their sewing-things on the table, and slipped their thimbles on to their fingers.

"Now, let me see, are we all here?" said Aunt Jemima. "Sally Simple, Dame Grumps, Lucy Lettuce, Mother Mangle, and Fanny Fickle. Yes. Well, we can set to work at once."

Now Sally Simple was sitting just underneath the lamp-shade, and on it Meddle had put two or three long red worms. He watched them from his hiding-place, hoping and hoping that they wouldn't wriggle off and fall on Sally.

Suddenly one long worm wriggled too far. It fell off the silk lamp-shade right on to Sally's head. Sally gave a scream and put up her hand to find out what was in her hair. When she felt the long worm she squealed and squealed.

"Sally! Sally! What's the matter?" cried every one in a fright.

"A worm dropped on me!" screamed Sally.

"Nonsense! Nonsense!" said Aunt Jemima at once. "How could a worm drop on you? Worms don't live in houses!"

A second worm dropped on Sally from the lamp-shade and she jumped up in fright. The third worm dropped on the table, and everybody jumped in horror.

"It *is* a worm!" said Mother Mangle. "And, oh, save us all, what's that crawling on that picture?"

Everybody looked—and they saw a big and furry caterpillar crawling

on the glass. Then Dame Grumps saw two beetles running along the mantelpiece, and she squealed loudly, for she was terribly afraid of beetles.

A fat caterpillar dropped on to Lucy Lettuce's hand, and she yelled for help. In half a minute every one was squealing and yelling, for they saw worms, beetles, and caterpillars everywhere. Then Aunt Jemima noticed her two frightened canaries hiding up on the top of the curtains. She hadn't noticed that they were out of their cage before, and she was very astonished.

"Jemima, this is a fine state for your room to be in for a sewing-meeting!" said Dame Grumps angrily. "I'm going! You may think it's a funny joke, but I *don't*!" She gathered

up her sewing-things and gave a scream — she had picked up a cater-pillar too!

She jumped so much that she sent her silver thimble flying out of her hand. It dropped on Meddle, who was trembling behind the sofa. Sally

Simple bent over the back of the sofa to pick up the thimble for Dame Grumps.

She saw Meddle's scared white face looking up at her, and she gave such a yell that Aunt Jemima dropped everything she was holding, and her scissors cut her foot.

"There's something behind the sofa!" yelled Sally.

"What is it? A worm? A beetle?" asked Lucy Lettuce. "Really, this is beyond a joke!"

"It's some sort of horrid big insect with a white ugly face," said Sally, and she sat down, plump, in a chair and fanned herself, feeling quite faint.

Well, in another moment Meddle was pulled out of his hiding-place, for as soon as Aunt Jemima spied him there she guessed all that had happened. She shook him till his teeth rattled.

"So *you* brought all these dreadful things into my house!" she said. "Meddling again! Didn't I tell you that my birds like seed and nothing else? You take all your creatures home with you, Meddle, and don't you dare to show your face in my house again unless you want a pail of cold water all over you!"

And she stuffed all the beetles, the caterpillars, and worms down poor Meddle's neck and turned him out of doors. How he wriggled! How he shook! It was dreadful to feel things wriggling and running all over him. One by one they fell out and ran or wriggled away, very glad to be free again. They had had a most unpleasant adventure — and, dear me, so had Meddle.

"I shan't try to do a good turn again," he said in a huff. Well — we shall see!

CHAPTER IX

MISTER MEDDLE GOES OUT TO STAY

Once Mister Meddle went to stay with Jitters, his cousin. He packed his bag and set off in a happy mood. Jitters had a nice house and garden —it would be fun to stay with him.

But when he got there, he found that Jitters was cross. "The fire is smoking," said Jitters. "I don't know how we are going to sit here and talk, Meddle. The smoke comes puffing out all the time and makes me choke."

"Put the fire out and I'll see if I can brush the soot away from the back of the chimney," said Meddle. "When my chimney smokes I just get my little brush and sweep the soot from the back—just there—and usually it is quite all right again."

"I don't think you'd better try to do that, Meddle," said Jitters at once. He knew what happened when Meddle interfered with anything!

But Meddle took no notice. He got a can of water and threw it on the fire to make it go out. It sizzled loudly, and sent such clouds of black smoke into the room that poor Jitters had to run out at once, coughing and choking.

"Now," said Meddle, taking up the brush that stood in the hearth, "I'll just show Jitters how clever I am at putting these little things right!"

He stuck the brush up the chimney and began to sweep. He swept a great

deal of soot down on himself, but he
didn't mind. After he had swept
away all he could find, he put his
head up the chimney to see if there
was any more he could reach – and
down came a whole pile right on to
his hair!

My goodness, that made Meddle

choke as if he had a hundred fish-bones stuck in his throat!

Jitters put his head in at the door and sighed when he saw the mess. "Come out, Meddle," he said. "You've made quite enough mess for to-day. I'll get the sweep in now."

Meddle was quite glad to leave the smoky, sooty room. He went into the drawing-room with Jitters and sat down in a chair. He leaned his head against a cushion.

Jitters saw the cushion turn black at once. He groaned. "Meddle," he said, "Do you mind going upstairs and having a bath and washing your hair? You will make all my chairs and cushions as black as can be. Do go, there's a good chap!"

Well, Meddle was always willing to do what any one wanted, so he got up at once. "Certainly, Jitters," he said. "I'll do it at once. What shall I wash my hair with?"

"There's a tin of shampoo-powder on the bathroom shelf," said Jitters. "Mix it in a glass, and it will make a fine lather. You can use that for your hair. There is plenty of hot water in the tap."

Meddle went upstairs, humming. It was rather fun to have a bath in the middle of the day. He turned on the taps. But unfortunately he was so long undressing that the bath overflowed on to the floor, and Meddle had to spend a long time wiping up the mess with a towel. It was a pity it was a nice clean towel, because it looked very dirty when he had finished!

Meddle got into the bath, which at once overflowed again. So he had to pull out the plug to let out some of the water—and, of course, he forgot to put it in again, so before he had sat in the bath two minutes, there was no water left!

"Oh, well, never mind!" said Meddle. "I'm getting cleaner now. I'll do my hair next."

He looked for the tin. There was one in a cupboard, so he took it out. He emptied some of the white powder inside into a glass and ran some water into it. It fizzed up splendidly.

"A beautiful lather!" said Meddle, and he emptied it all over his hair.

But the lather soon went, and left

his hair feeling very sticky indeed. Jitters put his head inside the door just then to find out how Meddle was getting on.

"All right, thank you," said Meddle. "But this shampoo-powder is rather funny, Jitters."

Jitters took up the tin. "This is a tin of my best sherbet-powder," he said sharply. "Do you usually wash your hair in sherbet, Meddle? What a sticky mess you'll be in!"

"Oh dear! I didn't look at the label," groaned Meddle. "Never mind—I'll soon get it right if you'll hand me the proper tin."

Jitters gave him the tin of shampoo-powder and shut the door with a bang. He was getting a bit tired of Meddle.

Meddle washed his hair clean. There was no soot left. "Well," said Meddle, pleased, "I really am getting very nice and clean now! I'll do my teeth too—my mouth feels very sooty."

But Meddle couldn't find his tube of tooth-paste when he looked in his bag. He had forgotten it. So

he looked in Jitters' cupboard again, and there he found a half-used tube. "Good!" said Meddle. "I'm sure Jitters won't mind me using a little."

He squeezed some out on to his toothbrush. It was a light-brown colour and smelt a bit funny. Meddle rubbed the brush on his teeth — round and about, and in and out. Then he set his teeth together and looked at them in the glass to see if they were clean.

"Nasty fishy taste this tooth-paste has," said Meddle to himself. "And, oh dear — my teeth are all brown now! I wonder if my tongue is, too."

He tried to open his teeth to look at his tongue, but, good gracious! he couldn't get them apart. They were stuck firmly together! In a panic

Meddle picked up the tube he had used and looked to see what was printed on it. "Best fish-glue," he read. "Will stick anything together —broken china, furniture, and so on."

Meddle groaned. He went to Jitters in dismay and showed him the tube, pointing to his teeth at the same time. Jitters laughed and laughed and laughed.

"Meddle! What will you do next?" he cried. "You wash your hair in sherbet, and you clean your teeth with glue! Well, you won't be able to eat or talk for a good while now, till the glue wears off. You will be a very easy visitor to have."

But Meddle wouldn't stop. He was very angry indeed to hear Jitters laughing. He fetched his bag, put on his hat back to front, and marched off to the bus.

But he couldn't ask for his ticket, so he had to walk all the way home. The glue wore off after a while, and Meddle could talk and eat; but he wouldn't eat fish for a long time after that because, he said, it tasted of glue!

CHAPTER X

MISTER MEDDLE AND THE SNOW

One morning when Mister Meddle got up he saw that it was snowing. Dear me, how it snowed! It snowed all night and it snowed all day.

"Just like great big goose-feathers coming down from the sky," said

Mister Meddle, as he watched the snowflakes falling.

He rattled the pennies in his pocket. Mister Meddle had four of them there—and that was all the money he had. It wouldn't buy very much. Somehow or other he must get some more.

"I think I'll go and see if any one wants their snow sweeping away," said Mister Meddle. "If I take my broom and my spade I might be able to earn quite a lot of money."

So he found his broom and his spade, and put them over his shoulder. Then off he went to find some work.

He came to Dame Fanny's cottage. She was at the window, looking up at the snow. Meddle called to her:

"Shall I sweep a path to your front door for you, Dame Fanny?"

"No, thank you!" called back Dame Fanny. "I don't trust you to do anything sensibly, Mister Meddle!"

Meddle was angry. Of course he could act sensibly! How rude of Dame Fanny! He would sweep a path just to show her how well he could work. So, as soon as the old dame had gone from the window, Mister Meddle set to work.

He couldn't seem to find the proper path, so he swept hard where he thought it was. After he had swept quite a long time Dame Fanny looked out of the window again — and, my goodness, how angry she was!

"You're sweeping across my beds!" she shouted. "All my snowdrops were coming up there — and now you have swept all their heads off! Look at them there in the snow, you mischievous creature! Just wait till I come out to you!"

But Meddle didn't wait! He shot off down the road as fast as his feet would take him. "How was I to know she was growing silly snowdrops all over the place!" he grumbled. "Oh, I say! Look at that great pile of snow by the side of the road there! How dreadful! I will dig it away and sweep it flat."

So he began. He dug his spade into the big heap of snow and threw it behind him. Then he swept it over the pavement, feeling very pleased to think that he had got rid of such a big heap of snow.

But he had hardly finished when Mister Biscuit the baker, outside whose shop the big heap of snow had stood, suddenly put his head out of his door.

"And what do you think *you* are doing?" he asked Mister Meddle, in a voice like ice.

"Oh, please, sir, I found a great heap of snow outside your shop, so I thought I'd better break it up and flatten it down on the pavement," said Meddle. "It was such a *big* heap of snow!"

"It was," said Mister Biscuit, in a horrid sort of voice. "I made it myself, Mister Meddle! I swept all the snow off my pavement, and packed it up into a big heap to melt—and now *you've* come along and undone all my work! The snow is all over my pavement again! Come here, you meddling, interfering little man!"

But Meddle didn't go to Mister Biscuit. No, he knew better than that! He skipped off down the road as if a dog was after him.

"I'm not really getting on very

well," said Mister Meddle sadly.
"Oh, look—what a lot of snow there
is outside Father Flap's house. He's
an old chap, so perhaps he would
like someone to dig it away for him."

So Meddle went up to the door
through the thick snow and knocked
on the knocker. Father Flap opened
the door. "What is it?" he growled.

"Father Flap, let me sweep away the snow from your garden," said Meddle. "I'm a good workman, I am. I'd be pleased to do it for sixpence."

"You're not a good workman, and I don't want it done!" said Father Flap. "I like the snow there. It looks pretty." He slammed his door shut.

Meddle sighed. He looked up at the roof and saw that the snow lay heavily there too. "That's really very dangerous," he said to himself. "That snow will slide down and bury someone if Father Flap's not careful."

Meddle opened the letter-box flap in the front door and shouted through it. "Hie! Shall I make your roof safe for you? There's a lot of snow there!"

There was no answer. Father Flap had gone into his warm kitchen and shut the door. Meddle stood on the snowy step and looked up at the roof.

"Well, if I clear the snow from there, perhaps Father Flap will pay me for it," he thought. "If I make it all clean, and push the snow off, surely he will give me sixpence."

So he stood on the water-barrel nearby and climbed up on to the roof. He clung to a chimney and began to kick at the snow with his feet to clear it from the roof.

Now Father Flap was sitting snoozing in his kitchen with Dame Flap when they suddenly heard a most peculiar noise on their roof. Of course, they had no idea that Meddle was there! They both sat up and looked at one another.

"Cats on the roof again!" said Dame Flap angrily. "Go and shoo them off, Flap; I will NOT have cats on my roof."

So Father Flap went to the front door and opened it. He walked out on the doorstep and looked up at the roof—and at that very moment Meddle loosened a great sheet of snow with his foot and it slid down with a swooshing sound. It fell off the roof straight on to poor Father Flap underneath! It buried him from head to foot, and he began to yell and shout.

Meddle climbed down the water-barrel to see what all the noise was about. He was most astonished to hear shouts coming from the snow he had pushed off—but when he saw

Father Flap's angry face suddenly looking out from the top, he guessed what had happened!

"Wait till I catch you, you meddlesome creature!" yelled Father Flap.

He struggled out of the snow and ran at Meddle—but Meddle rushed away. Up the hill behind the cottage he went, up and up, hoping that Father Flap would soon be out of breath. But Father Flap was strong, and he was so angry that he meant to catch Meddle whatever happened, if he ran to the end of the world.

When Meddle got to the top of the hill he stopped. The other side was too steep to run down. Whatever was he to do? Father Flap decided that for him! He caught poor Meddle, gave him a good shaking, and then pushed him down the steep side of the hill!

Over went Meddle into the deep snow—but he didn't stop there! Dear me, no! He couldn't stop, because the hill was so steep — so down he rolled, covered with snow.

And the farther he went, the more he was covered with snow, until at last he looked like a great snow-ball rolling down the hill! Over and over he rolled, getting bigger every moment.

At the bottom of the hill some children were playing. When they saw the enormous snowball coming down on top of them they ran off with squeals and screams. The great snowball, with Meddle inside, rolled to the bottom of the hill, and came to a stop in the middle of the frozen pond. There it lay on the ice, quite still, with poor Meddle inside trying to shout and wriggle.

He couldn't get out, and Father

Flap wasn't going to run down the hill and help him, so nobody bothered at all. And there he stayed until the sun came out and began to melt the snowball.

Meddle was so pleased. Soon he would be free again — but dear me, the sun melted the ice on the pond too! And by the time that Meddle got out of the snowball the ice had turned to water, and there was Meddle splashing in the cold, half-frozen pond!

"Whatever do you want to go bathing in the pond *this* time of year for?" shouted the village policeman. "Come on out quickly, Mister Meddle!"

Meddle came out, wet and cold. He went home and got himself a hot-water bottle and a cup of hot milk. He shook his head sadly at his old black cat who was waiting for him to give her the skin off the top of the milk.

"It's no good trying to do anything for anybody," said Meddle. "Not a bit of good, Pusskins."

Well, it all depends on how you set about it, doesn't it!

CHAPTER XI

MISTER MEDDLE GOES OUT SHOPPING

When Meddle was staying with his friend Giggle in Heyho Village, he met all the people there and liked them very much. They didn't know his meddling ways, and they liked him too. So Meddle felt very happy indeed.

"If only I could help them and show them what a clever, kindly chap I am!" thought Meddle. "At home nobody trusts me, and they all laugh at me. It's too bad."

Well, his chance came very soon. It happened that Mrs. Tilly, Mrs. Binks, and Miss Tubby all wanted to go for a morning's outing together, and they couldn't.

"What should I do with my baby if I went out for the morning?" sighed Mrs. Tilly.

"And who would do my shopping?" said Mrs. Binks.

"And who would take my dog for

a walk?" said Miss Tubby, who loved her little white dog very much.

Meddle was passing by, and he heard them talking. At once he swept off his hat, bowed low, and said, "Dear ladies, let me help you. I can take the baby out in its pram, do Mrs. Binks's shopping, and take the dog for a walk all at the same time! Pray let me do this for you!"

"Oh, thank you," said Mrs. Tilly, beaming at Mister Meddle. "It *would* be kind of you to help us."

She didn't know that Meddle loved meddling and that things always went wrong with him! She led him to where her baby lay asleep in its pram. It was a pretty, golden-haired child with fat little hands.

"There's little Peterkin," she said.

"Now if you'll just keep an eye on him for me, he'll be all right."

"And here's my shopping list," said Mrs. Binks, giving him a long list.

"Thank you," said Meddle. He put the list into his pocket. "And now let me have your dog," he said to Miss Tubby.

Miss Tubby gave him her dog's lead. "His name is Spot," she said. "Do you see his big black spot? He is such a darling little dog."

The dog growled at Meddle. Meddle took the lead, and thought that the dog didn't sound a darling at all.

"Well, thank you, dear Mister Meddle," said the three women, and they nodded at him and then went off for their morning's outing.

Meddle felt very proud. What a lot of help he was giving, to be sure!

"I'll walk down to the village now," he said to himself. "I can wheel the pram, and hold the dog's lead in my hand to make the dog come along too — and I will go to the grocer's and get all the things that Mrs. Binks wants."

So off he went, wheeling the pram, and dragging along the dog, who didn't seem to want to come a bit! Soon he met his friend, Mister Giggle, who stared in amazement.

"Whatever are you doing, Meddle?" he said. "Where did you get that baby from — and the dog?"

"I'm helping people a bit, Giggle," said Meddle. "I'll be in to dinner all right. I've just promised to mind this baby and this dog and do a spot of shopping."

Giggle began to laugh. Meddle looked offended and walked off, pushing the pram and dragging the dog. Soon he came to the grocer's shop. He went inside, first putting the pram against the shop window, and

tying the dog to a post. He pulled a list from his pocket.

Silly old Meddle! It wasn't Mrs. Binks's list at all! It was a list he had made out for himself three weeks before — but Meddle didn't think of that. He thought it was the right one, of course.

He ordered all the things on the list. They were what he had ordered just before he gave a party. "One pound of chocolate biscuits," said Meddle. "Two pounds of best butter. Two-pound pot of strawberry jam. One pound of shortbread, and two bottles of lemonade."

That was all there was on the list. Meddle looked at it, feeling a little surprised. "I thought it was a longer list," he said. "I must have been

wrong about that."

The grocer put all the things into Meddle's net-bag. Outside went Meddle, and walked to the first pram he saw. It wasn't Mrs. Tilly's pram at all, nor her baby either! Somebody else had put their pram outside the shop since Meddle had put his, but dear old Meddle didn't think of that! He didn't even look at the baby inside. If he had he would have seen that it was a dark-haired little girl, not a golden-haired baby boy!

Meddle hung his bag on the pram-handle, put off the brake on the pram, and started for home. He hadn't gone very far when he remembered the dog! He had left it behind.

"Bother!" said Meddle. "Oh, bother! Now I must go back to fetch it!"

So back he went, pushing the pram. "Let me see, what was that dog like?" wondered Meddle, trying to remember. "Oh yes — it was called Spot. It has a spot on its coat."

He walked back to the grocer's, and when he was nearly there a large dog met him. "Hallo," said Meddle, staring at him. "You've got a spot on your back. You must be Spot!"

The dog wagged his tail. His name *was* Spot. Most dogs with spots on their back seem to be called Spot, and this dog was a very friendly one, willing to go to anyone who said his name.

"So you *are* Spot!" said Meddle. "Where's your lead, you bad dog?"

"Woof, woof!" said the dog, gambolling round Meddle.

"You've lost that lead of yours, Spot," said Meddle sternly. "What do you suppose Miss Tubby will say to you?"

"Woof, woof!" said the dog again, not knowing at all who Miss Tubby was.

"Come here, sir," said Meddle, and he caught the dog by the collar. He slipped a string through it and tied the dog to the pram-handle. Then off he went again. He took the baby for a long walk, and then went back to Mrs. Tilly's garden to wait for her to return.

He sat there, reading, very pleased with himself. If only the people in his own village could see how folk here trusted him with their babies and dogs and shopping! Ha, they would be sorry they had ever laughed at him.

At twenty minutes to one Mrs. Tilly, Mrs. Binks, and Miss Tubby came back. They went into the garden and smiled at Meddle, who jumped up at once and bowed politely.

Mrs. Tilly looked at the pram, and gave a jump. She went very red and stared at Meddle.

"Where's my baby?" she said.

"In the pram, of course, sweet little thing!" said Meddle, gazing fondly at the sleeping baby. He was a little astonished to see a dark one—surely the other had been fair?

"Meddle, this is *not* my baby!" said Mrs. Tilly, looking like a fierce mother-cat all of a sudden. "And this is not my pram either, though it is dark-blue like mine. WHAT HAVE YOU DONE WITH MY BABY?"

She looked so very fierce that Meddle was frightened. He took a step backwards and fell over the dog. The dog growled.

"Be quiet, Spot," said Meddle. "How dare you trip me up?"

"*That's* not Spot," said Miss Tubby. "My dog is little and white with a black spot. This one is large and black with a white spot! WHAT HAVE YOU DONE WITH MY DOG?"

"Not your dog?" said Meddle, looking at the dog in surprise. "Well, but he must be. How could a dog change like that? And how could a baby change either? You must have forgotten what your baby looked like, Mrs. Tilly, and you must have forgotten your dog, Miss Tubby."

"And what about my shopping?" said Mrs. Binks, looking at the net-bag. "Do you suppose that is what was on my list, Meddle?"

"Certainly," said Meddle, opening the bag. "Biscuits, lemonade, short-bread, butter . . ."

"I didn't put *any* of those on my list!" said Mrs. Binks angrily. "This is just a horrid joke you are playing on us, Meddle. Well, I won't pay you for those things—you can pay for them yourself, and take them home!"

159

Just then there was a scraping at the front gate and in came the right Spot, dragging his lead behind him! He had managed to get free! Miss Tubby ran to him and hugged him.

"So here you are!" she said. "Did that wicked Meddle leave you behind, poor darling! You can bite him if you like, the horrid fellow!"

"Grrrrrrrrr!" said Spot, showing his teeth at poor Meddle. Meddle made up his mind to go—if only he could slip out without being noticed! But Spot wouldn't let him go. He stood by the gate, growling!

Suddenly someone came hurrying down the road with a dark-blue pram. She saw Mrs. Tilly and called to her. "Mrs. Tilly! I've lost my baby! I found yours alone outside the grocer's

shop, and I wondered if some one had taken mine instead. So I've brought yours for you—have you got mine?"

"Oh yes, I have!" cried Mrs. Tilly joyfully. She rushed to her baby, and took it out of its pram, talking lovingly to it. Meddle thought it would be a good time to get out of the gate.

But just as he was going, Spot rushed at him and bit a big hole in his trousers! Mrs. Binks picked a tomato from a nearby plant and threw it at him—splosh!—and Mrs. Tilly called out that she would get a policeman because he had stolen someone else's baby!

Poor Meddle! He ran back to Mister Giggle's in a hurry. He fetched his bag. He wouldn't even stop to eat his dinner. He caught the first bus home —and went into his house with the biscuits, shortbread, lemonade, jam, and butter.

"I'm a most unlucky fellow," he said sadly, as he spread butter on the biscuits, and poured out some lemonade. "A most unlucky fellow!"

CHAPTER XII

MISTER MEDDLE DRIVES THE TRAIN

One day, when Mister Meddle was walking beside the railway line, he saw a train standing quite still beside a signal.

There was nobody inside the driving-cab of the engine. Nobody at all.

"Very queer," said Meddle, looking at the empty cab in surprise. "Most peculiar. I can't understand it."

There were plenty of people *in* the train. "All waiting to go on their journey, and nobody to drive them," said Meddle. "Dear, dear, whatever are things coming to?"

He walked across the lines to the

train. He climbed into the cab of the engine and had a good look at everything there. He had always wanted to see the inside of an engine cab.

"I can't imagine why the driver and the stoker are not here," said Meddle.

If he had only looked out on the other side he would have seen that the driver and stoker were busy picking the ripe blackberries that grew on the hedge there. They knew they had five minutes to wait before the signal went down, and they were having a nice time with the blackberries!

Well, you can guess what Meddle did! He touched this handle, and he pushed that one. He poked here and he poked there.

And suddenly he pulled a handle that started the engine! Oh, Meddle, Meddle, you are a dreadful fellow, really!

"Chuff-chuff-chuff!" The engine ran along the lines. The driver and the stoker jumped with surprise and dismay. They saw their train running away from them! They gave a shout

and tore after it as fast as ever they could.

But they couldn't catch it. It went too fast. At first Meddle was frightened when the train began to go. He wondered if he should jump out — but when he saw how fast the hedges flew by, he didn't dare to jump.

"Perhaps I can stop the train," he thought. So he began to try all the different handles.

One let off the steam — "Eeeeeeee-eee!" whistled the engine, and Meddle jumped so much at the sudden noise that he almost fell off the train.

The train rushed through a station. It usually stopped there, and the stationmaster got the surprise of his life when he saw it rushing through. Whatever was happening?

Meddle pulled another handle. The train slowed down. "Good," said Meddle; "now perhaps it will stop." But it didn't, so he pulled the handle next to the stop-handle, and turned a wheel too, just for luck.

The engine began to puff very fast, and tore along as if something was chasing it! Oh dear, oh dear, it was a most terrifying ride!

People in the carriages began to put their heads out of the windows, wondering what in the world was happening to their train. They didn't like the way it behaved at all!

Meddle set the whistle going again by mistake. "EeeeeeeeeEEEEEE-EEE!" shrieked the train, and tore through another station.

Then it went into a long tunnel,

and Meddle couldn't see a thing.

When the train came out into the sunshine again Meddle looked out through the cab-window to see if there was another station coming. But to his great dismay he saw that he was coming to the end of the railway line!

"Oh, goodness!" said Meddle. "Whatever am I to do? I don't know how to stop the train! It will bang right into the buffers—crash!"

So he began to pull every handle he could see, and he turned every wheel this way and that. The poor engine didn't know what to do. How could it go slow and fast at once? How could it stop, and go full speed at the same time?

It began to rock like a rocking-

horse, because Meddle had pulled down the handle for "Go Backwards" and the one for "Go Forwards" too. So the engine was trying to go forwards and backwards at the same time, and rocked like a boat in a stormy sea! It was dreadful.

It came to the buffers. It crashed

through them. It leapt into the air, and then rushed forwards again — but not on the lines this time, because there were now no lines to run on. They stopped at the buffers.

The carriages caught against the buffers and broke away from the engine. The people all got out in a hurry, glad to be safe. They looked for their engine.

Dear me, whatever had happened to it? It had rushed over a field, and had come to the river. It had plunged straight into the water, and its big fire had gone out with a sizzling noise: "S-s-s-s-s-s-s-s!"

And where was Meddle. He was sitting on top of the funnel, which was still puffing out hot smoke. He had been thrown there when the engine jumped into the river. It was a most uncomfortable place, because for one thing it was terribly hot, and for another thing the smoke nearly choked him.

"Save me, save me!" cried Meddle. Some swans swam up in surprise. They were angry because this enormous puffing monster had dived into their river. They pecked Meddle hard, and he yelled:

"Don't! Don't! Oh, save me, some one, save me!"

A great crowd came on to the river bank. All the people talked at once. How were they to get the engine out of the river?

Just then a showman came by with two elephants, on his way to a circus. When he saw what the trouble was he offered to let his elephants pull the engine out of the water. So two ropes were fetched, and the elephants pulled hard at their ends. The other ends of the rope were fastened to the funnel by Meddle.

With a jerk the engine came out of the river, dripping wet. And just as it was hauled safely up the bank, with Meddle still hanging on to the funnel, up came the engine-driver and the stoker! They had run all the way after their beloved train!

"How dare you run away with our train?" yelled the driver.

"I didn't know it was yours," said Meddle. "I didn't see you. I thought the engine-cab was quite empty."

"You're a tiresome, meddlesome creature," said the stoker. "And you

can just come back to the engine-yard with us and clean our engine from top to bottom! It is all muddy and wet! That will keep you busy for quite a long time, dear Mister Meddle!"

Meddle hasn't been home for two weeks now. He is still busy cleaning that big engine. He hasn't done so much hard work for ages, and he has quite made up his mind that he will never, never drive an engine again!

CHAPTER XIII

MISTER MEDDLE AND THE CLOCK

Once it happened that a bird began to make its nest inside the village hall clock. The clock always told the time to the people of the village, and it could easily be·seen on the tower of the hall.

Meddle happened to be in the village hall when the bird's nest was seen. There was going to be a concert that night, and Meddle and some others were putting a great many chairs into rows ready for the night.

Every time that Meddle passed underneath the back of the clock, he heard a tweeting noise, and at last he looked up. A little bird sat there, holding a straw in its beak.

"Look at that!" said Meddle. "There's a bird building its nest inside the clock. Naughty, naughty!"

"Tweet!" said the bird, and that was all the notice it took of Meddle.

"What shall we do about it?" asked Mistress Fanny. "It will stop the clock altogether if we let the bird build there. We had better get Mister Tock the clockmaker to come and see to it."

"Oh, dear me, why bother to fetch Mister Tock!" said Meddle at once. "*I* could get that bird's nest out quite easily, and shoo the bird away too."

"You'd better not meddle with it," said Dame Flap. "You always manage to get into mischief when you do, Meddle."

Meddle pretended he hadn't heard what Dame Flap had said. He bustled about to find a ladder. But there wasn't one.

So he built up five chairs, all balanced on one another. They just reached below the clock. Meddle began to climb up. Good gracious! It did look dangerous.

"He thinks he's a clown at a circus or something," whispered Dame Flap. "I know he'll fall! Serve him right for meddling!"

Meddle reached the clock safely. He found out where the bird got in and out. It was a tiny hole at the side of the clock's works. Meddle found the door that opened the back of the clock.

He opened the door, and looked inside. Dear, dear! The bird had built quite half its nest already! The clock would have stopped by the next night, Meddle was sure.

He began to clear out the straw, dead leaves, and moss. He didn't look at all where he was throwing it, of course, and it went all over the people below. They were very cross.

"Straw all over my hair!" said Dame Flap.

"Moss down my neck!" said Mistress Fanny. "That tiresome Meddle!"

The little bird suddenly saw what Meddle was doing and flew at him in rage. Meddle got a hard peck on his nose, and he was most annoyed. He nearly fell off the pile of chairs.

"Go away! Shoo! Shoo!" he shouted to the bird. But the bird wouldn't be shooed, and it flew again at Meddle. Meddle put up his hand to protect his eyes, and his sleeve caught in the works of the clock. He dragged his sleeve away, and as he did so he made the hands of the clock go round very quickly, so that they pointed to half-past twelve instead of to half-past eleven! Meddle didn't know that, of course — he couldn't see the clock face outside the hall.

The bird flew away, tweeting. Meddle tried to smack it as it went. He lost his balance — the chairs began to topple over — and down went Meddle and the chairs with a crash, smash, bang! Goodness, what a bump he got!

He picked himself up and dusted himself down. He was very angry indeed. He took one look at the laughing people and then walked out of the hall in a huff.

And then, what a to-do there was in the village. The big clock was the one that nearly every one used for the time. The people were always popping in and out of their houses to

see what the time was by the clock.

"Good gracious! It's dinner-time and my pudding isn't made yet!" cried Mother Fiddle, and she hurried up so much that her dinner was quite spoilt.

"Look at the time!" cried Mister Gobby, as he hurried by. "I'll never have time to get my dinner to-day before it's time to go back to work! What *has* happened to the morning?"

All the children were scolded for being late. They simply couldn't understand why the morning had seemed so short. They didn't guess that Mister Meddle had put the clock on a whole hour by mistake!

People had to wait ages for the bus that afternoon, because they were at the stopping-place a whole hour early. They scolded the bus-driver, and he couldn't understand it at all!

"It can't be four o'clock," he said, looking at the clock. "Dear, dear, I thought it was only three. What a long time I have been getting here today. I'm very sorry, folks."

The children all went to bed a whole hour early. The sun went down an hour too late, it seemed to every one! People were in a real muddle.

And then Mister Plod the policeman, who couldn't understand it either, had a good idea.

"The sun *can't* be wrong!" he said. "I shall put on my wireless set and get the right time-signal." So he did, and soon found that the village clock was a whole hour fast. Such a thing had never happened before!

"WHO has been fiddling with the village clock?" cried Mister Plod, in a great rage.

"Mister Meddle, of course," said Dame Flap. "He wouldn't let us fetch Mister Tock the clockmaker to put the bird's nest out of the works. He *would* do it himself.''

Well, Mister Tock was fetched to put the clock right. He had to get a ladder and put it up outside the village hall. He found it very difficult to put the clock right, for when Mister Meddle had caught his sleeve in the works, he had let a lot of straw drop down into the middle of the clock.

So Mister Tock had to look inside the clock as well as put the hands right outside. "This will cost five shillings,'' he told Mister Plod.

And who had to pay the bill? Yes, poor old Meddle, of course! Well, you really *would* think he'd give up interfering with things, wouldn't you? But I don't expect he ever will!